Oi AaRDVARK!

Written by
Kes Gray

Illustrated by
Jim Field

Hodder
Children's
Books

"Oi AaRDVARK!"

said the frog.

"Come and be in my new book!"

"It's called **MY ALL-NEW ALPHABETTY BOTTY BOOK**," said the frog. "It's for animals I haven't told where to sit yet, I'm going to start with **A** for Aardvark and then go all the way up to **Z!**"

"Good luck with that!" laughed the cat.

"What will **aardvarks** sit on?" asked the dog.

Aa

"**Aardvarks** will sit on **cardsharks!**" said the frog.

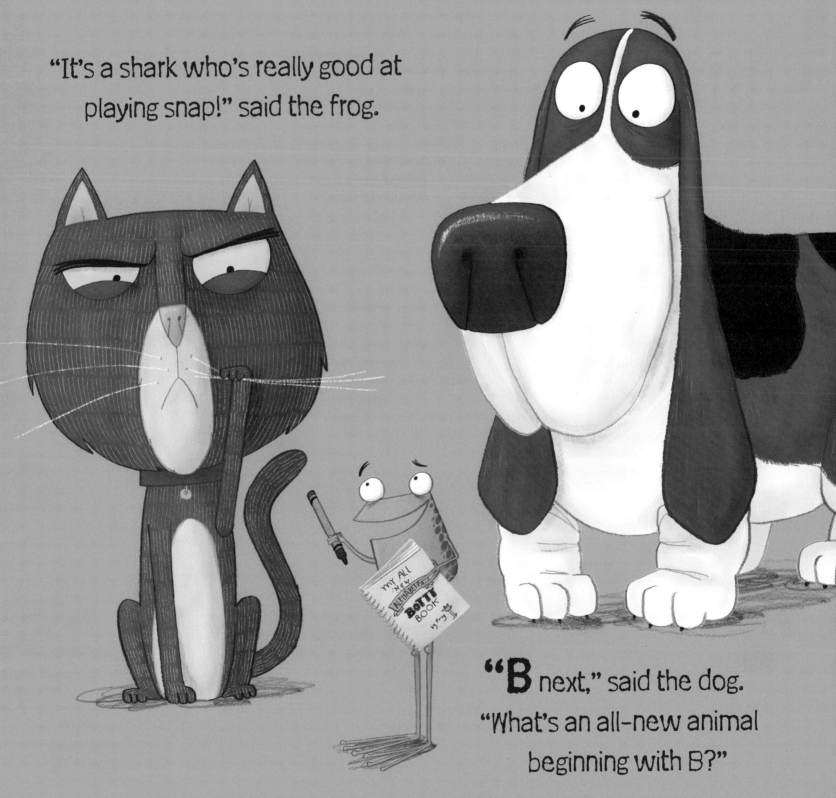

"What's a cardshark?" frowned the cat.

"It's a shark who's really good at playing snap!" said the frog.

"**B** next," said the dog. "What's an all-new animal beginning with B?"

Bb

"**Baboon!**" said the frog.

"**Baboons** can sit on **balloons!**

C c

And **crocs** can sit on **clocks!**"

"D next!" said the cat, "now you need to think of an **all-new D.**"

DOG! said the dog.

"**D** definitely begins with dog!"

"D doesn't begin with dog. **Dog** begins with D," frowned the cat, "and anyway, we've done dog before!"

Dd

"We haven't done **donkey!**" said the frog. **"Donkeys** can sit on **long keys!**"

"I wonder what **eels** could sit on?" said the cat.

E e

"**Eels** can sit on **reels**," said the frog,

"**elks** can sit on **whelks**,

Ff

finches
can sit on
winches,

Gg

giraffes
can sit on **baths**

and **gazelles**
can sit on **bells!"**

"I wonder what **horses** could sit on?"
said the dog.

Hh

"Horses can sit on **golf courses,"** said the frog.

"Horses can sit on **golf courses**

Ii

and **iguanas** can sit on **piranhas.**"

"**J** and **K** next," said the cat.

J j

"**Jays** can sit on **maize**," said the frog.

"**Jays** can sit on **maize**, **jerboas** can sit on **mowers**

Ll

"Llamas
will sit on
pyjamas

and lynx will sit
on drinks!"

"Frog's really good at writing alphabetty botty books,
isn't he?" said the dog.

"He hasn't got to **Z** yet," said the cat.

Mm

"**Mosquitos** will sit on **burritos**,

Nn

nits will sit on **banana splits,**

Oo

otters will sit on **swatters**

and **orcas** will sit on **piggy porkers,"** said the frog.

"Frog's BRILLIANT at this!" said the dog.

"Wait till you hear my new **P**s!" boasted the frog.

Ss

a **squid**
can sit on a **lid,**

Tt

turtles
can sit on
spurtles,

Qq

"Quetzels
will sit on
pretzels,

quolls will sit
on **holes.**

Rr

Racoons
will sit on
macaroons,

P p

"Possums
will sit on
blossoms,

pigeons
will sit on **wigeons,**

pangolins
will sit on
mandolins

and **pandas** will sit on **verandahs!**"

"You'll never think of a **Q**," said the cat.

LIFT THE FLAPS!

Vipers
will sit on **wipers**

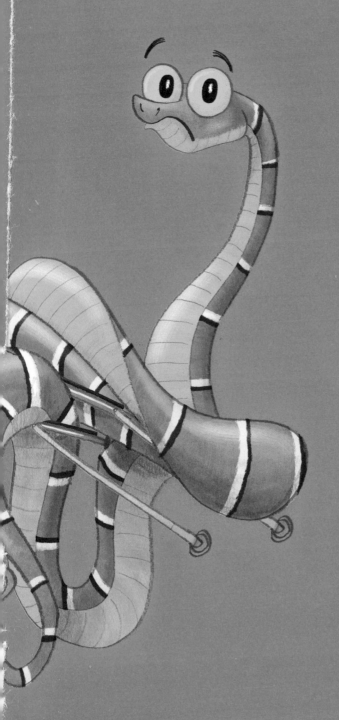

Ww and
wombats
will sit on
combats."

"Good luck with **X**," purred the cat.

ticks
can sit on
wicks,

Uu

uakaris will sit on **saris.**

Vv

X x

"X-ray tetra will sit on seabeds, seaweed, seashells, coral, shipwrecks **et cetera!"** clapped the frog.

Yy

"Yaks
will sit on **sacks,**

and just to prove I CAN even think of a **Z** ... **zebras** will now sit on ...

"What are *they* then...?"
asked the dog.

The artwork for this book was made during the lockdown of the Covid 19 outbreak. I'd like to dedicate this book to the doctors, nurses, volunteers, shop-workers and delivery drivers who put their lives at risk to save and help others. Thank you! J.F.

To normality! K.G.

HODDER CHILDREN'S BOOKS
First published in Great Britain in 2020 by
Hodder and Stoughton

Text copyright © Kes Gray, 2020
Illustrations copyright © Jim Field, 2020

The moral rights of the author and
illustrator have been asserted.
All rights reserved

A CIP catalogue record for this book is
available from the British Library.

ISBN: 978 1 444 95591 0

10 9 8 7 6 5 4 3 2 1

Printed and bound in Italy

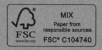
MIX
Paper from
responsible sources
FSC® C104740

Hodder Children's Books
An imprint of Hachette Children's Group
Part of Hodder and Stoughton
Carmelite House, 50 Victoria Embankment
London, EC4Y 0DZ

An Hachette UK Company
www.hachette.co.uk
www.hachettechildrens.co.uk

www.kesgray.com
www.jimfield.co.uk